A First-Start® Easy Reader

This easy reader contains only 56 different words,
repeated often to help the young reader develop
word recognition and interest in reading.

Basic word list for *Mike's First Haircut*

a	I	rather
and	is	really
asks	it	says
be	like	see
but	long	she
cannot	longer	short
cut	look	soon
day	looks	that
does	man	the
ears	me	this
every	Mike	time
eyes	Mike's	too
for	Mother	was
grows	my	who
hair	no	what
haircut	not	will
hear	oh	would
his	over	your
how	please	

Mike's First Haircut

Written by Sharon Gordon

Illustrated by Gioia Fiammenghi

Troll Associates

Library of Congress Cataloging in Publication Data

Gordon, Sharon.
    Mike's first haircut.

    Summary: Mike is afraid of what he will look like
after getting his first haircut.
    [1. Haircutting—Fiction] I. Fiammenghi, Gioia,
ill. II. Title.
PZ7.G65936Mi   1988   [E]   87-10911
ISBN 0-8167-1113-5 (lib. bdg.)
ISBN 0-8167-1114-3 (pbk.)

This is Mike.

Mike's hair is short.

But it grows every day.

It grows longer

and longer.

It grows over his eyes.

It grows over his ears.

Soon, Mike cannot hear.

And Mike cannot see.

"Time for a haircut," says Mother.

"Your hair is too long," she says.

"A haircut?

Who, me?"

"What will it be?"

"How will it look?"

"Like this? Oh no, please!"

"Like that? Oh no, please!"

"Oh please, not a haircut for me!"

"I would rather not hear.
I would rather not see!"

It was time for a haircut.

Mike's hair was too long.

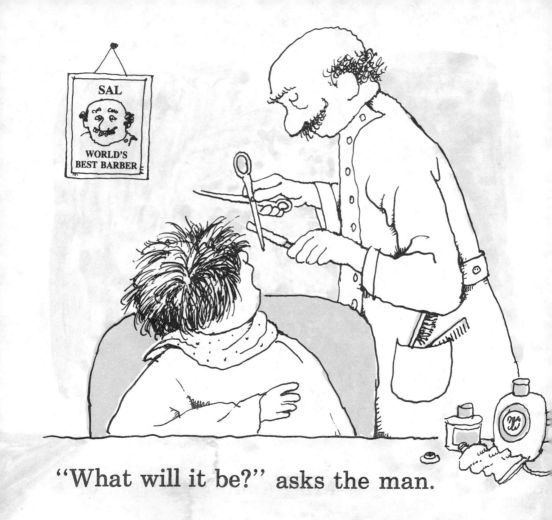

"What will it be?" asks the man.

"Cut it short," says Mother.

"How does it look?" asks the man.

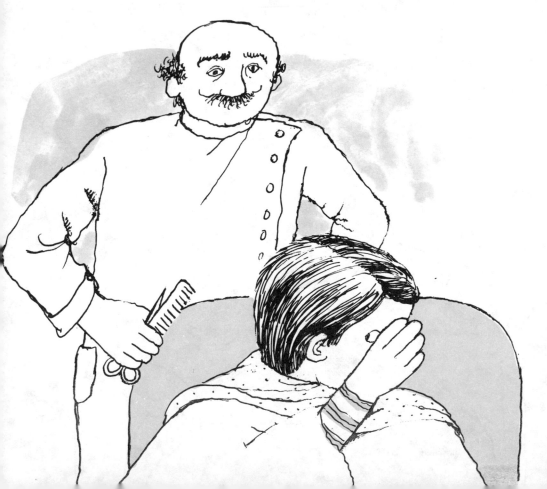

"Is that really *me*?" asks Mike.

"My haircut looks . . . like me!"